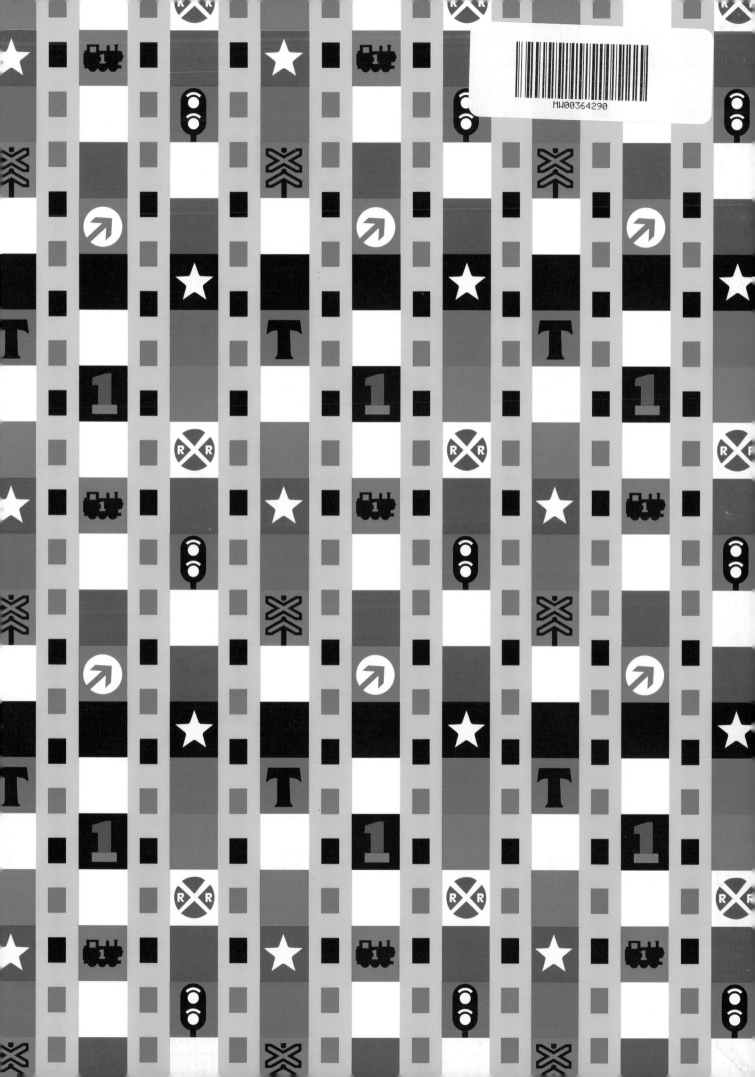

MW00364290

THOMAS & FRIENDS™

ANNUAL 2023

This annual belongs to:

....

....

Age:

....

First published in Great Britain 2022 by Farshore
An imprint of HarperCollins*Publishers*
1 London Bridge Street, London SE1 9GF
www.farshore.co.uk

HarperCollins*Publishers*
1st Floor, Watermarque Building, Ringsend Road, Dublin 4, Ireland

Written by Laura Jackson

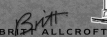

CREATED BY BRITT ALLCROFT

Based on the Railway Series by The Reverend W Awdry.
©2022 Gullane (Thomas) Limited. Thomas the Tank Engine & Friends™
and Thomas & Friends™ are trademarks of Gullane (Thomas) Limited.
©2022 HIT Entertainment Limited. HIT and the HIT logo are trademarks
of HIT Entertainment Limited.

ISBN 978 0 0085 0766 4
Printed in Romania
001

A CIP catalogue record for this title is available from the British Library.

All rights reserved. No part of this publication may be reproduced,
stored in a retrieval system, or transmitted, in any form or by any
means, electronic, mechanical, photocopying, recording or otherwise,
without the prior permission of the publisher and copyright owner.

Parental guidance is advised for all craft and colouring activities.
Always ask an adult to help when using glue, paint and scissors.
Wear protective clothing and cover surfaces to avoid staining.

Stay safe online.
Farshore is not responsible for content hosted by third parties.

MIX
Paper from
responsible sources
FSC® C007454

What's Inside?

Christmas Spot

Ho-ho-ho! It's Christmas on Sodor.
Can you find the festive friends and
fun items in the big picture?

Can you spot ... ?

*Shout out 'Happy Christmas!'
each time you spot one.*

Super Sizes

There are so many different sizes on Sodor. Take the quiz to show Sir Topham Hatt how much you know about sizes.

1 Point to the **TALLEST** friend.

2 Point to the **SMALLEST** animal.

3 Point to the **LONGEST** sea creature.

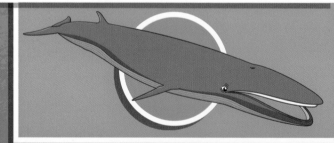  

Draw the longest thing you can imagine here.

Draw the teeniest-tiniest thing you can imagine here.

Rainy Rescue

Uh oh! Emily is stuck in a big storm.
Guide Rebecca through the maze to the rainy rescue.

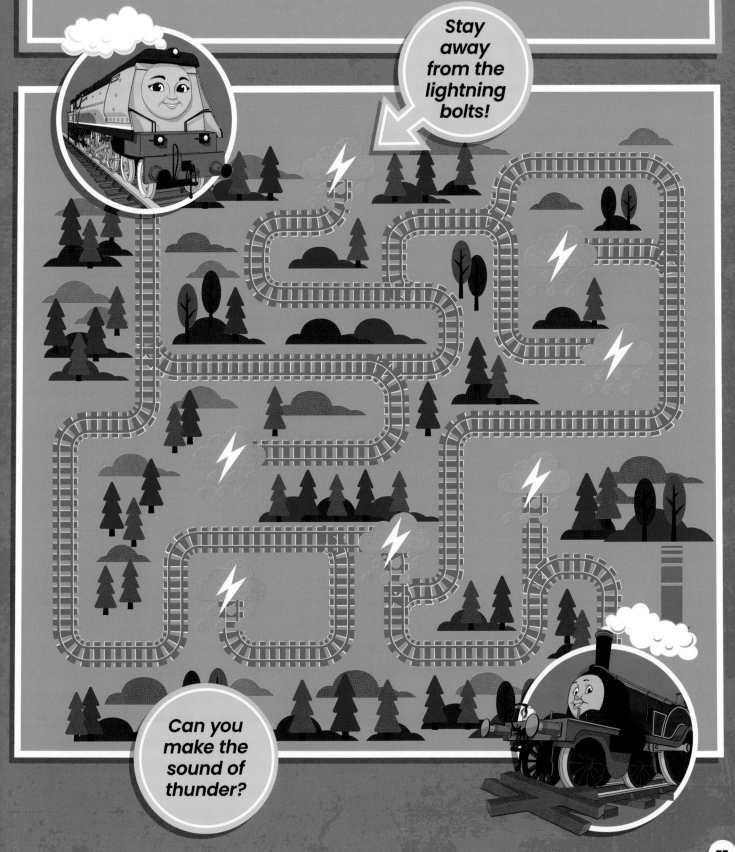

Into the Tunnel

Toot, toot! Here comes the tunnel!
When it all goes dark, can you still spot the engines?
Shout out the name of each engine.

1

2

3

4

Use this panel to help you.

EMILY

REBECCA

THOMAS

PERCY

Race a Friend

Challenge a friend and race to the finish line.
Choose who is going to be Nia and who is going
to be Thomas.

NIA

THOMAS

START

Now grab a pencil and race down the tracks. First one to their flag is the winner.

FINISH

Thomas' Fuzzy Friend

It was a sunny day on the Island of Sodor. Thomas, Nia and James had pulled into Knapford Station, when they heard a strange noise.

Ruff, ruff! A little dog was sitting on the tracks.

"A doggy!" puffed Nia. "Maybe it's lost, poor thing."

Thomas wanted to help, but the dog quickly scampered away.

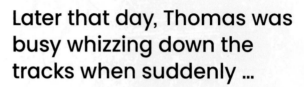

Later that day, Thomas was busy whizzing down the tracks when suddenly ...

Ruff, ruff! The little dog jumped onto the line again.

"You can't play on the tracks, doggy," Thomas gasped.

The dog wagged its tail. Thomas smiled. "Come on, hop on board. I'll help you find your home."

"Engines can't have pets, Thomas," warned Annie. "Pets are a big responsibility ..."

But the little dog had already jumped into the cabin. **Ruff!**

Clickety-clack, clickety-clack!

Thomas and the dog were soon **whizzing** and **whooshing** all around Sodor. Thomas **puffed** and **chuffed** all day long, but he couldn't find a home for the dog anywhere.

"Don't worry, I won't give up," puffed Thomas.

The doggy wasn't even listening. It had spied a squirrel in the distance.

Ruff! Quick as a flash, the dog jumped out of the cab and chased the squirrel down the tracks.

"No! Come back!" Thomas called out. He pumped his pistons and steamed after the runaway dog.

Faster, faster, faster!

"Doggy, doggy!" puffed Thomas.

Bumpity-bump-bump. The track ahead was old and bumpy. Thomas didn't notice a big branch ahead ...

CRASH!

Thomas rocked and rolled and skidded right off the track.

Uh oh. Poor Thomas was completely stuck.

Ruff! The little dog grabbed the driver's hat and scampered down the tracks again.

"**Wheesh!**" Thomas puffed. "Looking after a dog is hard work."

Little did Thomas know that the little dog was off on an important mission. A mission to rescue Thomas!

Later that day,
Sir Topham Hatt was
busy talking to a family,
when he heard a noise.

Ruff, ruff!

The little dog had found
its way back to Knapford
Station.

"That's my doggy!" the
little boy gasped. "Fuzzy!"

"Ah, so that is your dog," smiled Sir Topham Hatt.
Then he noticed the hat in the dog's mouth.
"Hang on, isn't that Thomas' driver's hat?"

Ruff! barked the dog.

"Is Thomas in trouble?" he asked the dog. **Ruff, ruff!**

"Right, we need to follow that dog!" said Sir Topham Hatt.

The dog took
Sir Topham Hatt
all the way to
Thomas.

"What a clever
doggy!"
Thomas cried
out when the
dog arrived
with help.

In no time at all, Thomas was safely back at Knapford Station.

"Sorry for the fuss," blushed Thomas. "I just wanted to help the doggy."

Sir Topham Hatt smiled. "It looks like it found its home after all."

The family on the platform hugged their dog.

"Dogs are a big responsibility," Thomas said to the little boy.

"I'll never lose my Fuzzy again!" said the boy.

Thomas was happy the dog had found his home again. He was also happy to have a rest. Looking after animals was hard work!

Ruff! Ruff!

Story Quiz

Now you have read along with Thomas' Fuzzy Friend, take the story quiz. Circle your answers.

1 What animal is Thomas trying to help?

dog

monkey

2 What does Thomas crash into on the tracks?

branch

Cranky

snowman

3 What does the dog chase down the tracks?

Bertie

squirrel

frog

4 Who takes the dog home?

Little boy

Sir Topham Hatt

Thomas

Now go back to the story and see how many questions you got right.

Answers on page 69.

Happy Chuff-mas!

Gordon has just delivered a big Christmas tree, but it's looking a bit bare. Trace over the lines and doodle lights and decorations to give it some magic.

Now draw a present for Gordon under the tree!

Go Green

Percy is a little engine who loves all things green!
Help Percy circle all the GREEN things in the big picture.

Now draw three more green
things here, just for Percy!

Answers on page 69.

Funny Faces

Thomas is feeling lots of emotions today.
Point to all the different faces Thomas is pulling.

happy

sad

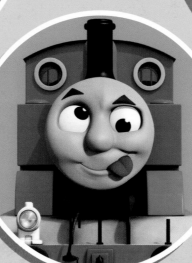

silly

cross

Now have
fun pulling
these faces
yourself!

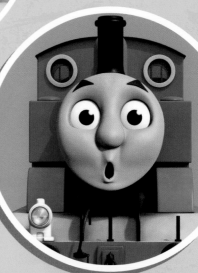

shocked

Dream Team

Sir Topham Hatt is very proud of the Steam Team. Use a pencil to trace over the words all about Sodor's top engines.

strong   kind

fun   brave

Can you think of any more words about the Steam Team?
Say them out loud!

Colour in your badge when you have finished.

1

Well done!

Very Important Engine

Use the little picture as a guide to colour in the big picture of Thomas. Then learn all about the different parts of the Number 1 Engine.

Colours to use:

Funnel to let out steam

Dome

Whistles

Buffers for pushing trucks

Coupling for pulling trucks

Wheels

Delivery Dash

It's Christmas Eve and there are lots of presents to deliver. Play the game and race a friend through Sodor to Santa.

YOU WILL NEED:

- 2-4 players
- a dice
- counters, such as coins or pieces of paper

HOW TO PLAY:

- Choose which engine you want to play.
- The youngest player rolls the dice first. Move the number of spaces that match the number rolled.
- If you land on the pictures, follow these instructions:

move forward two spaces

go back two spaces

take the short cut!

- The first one to Santa is the winner.

FINISH

30

29

17

18

19

16

15

14

13

START

1

2

3

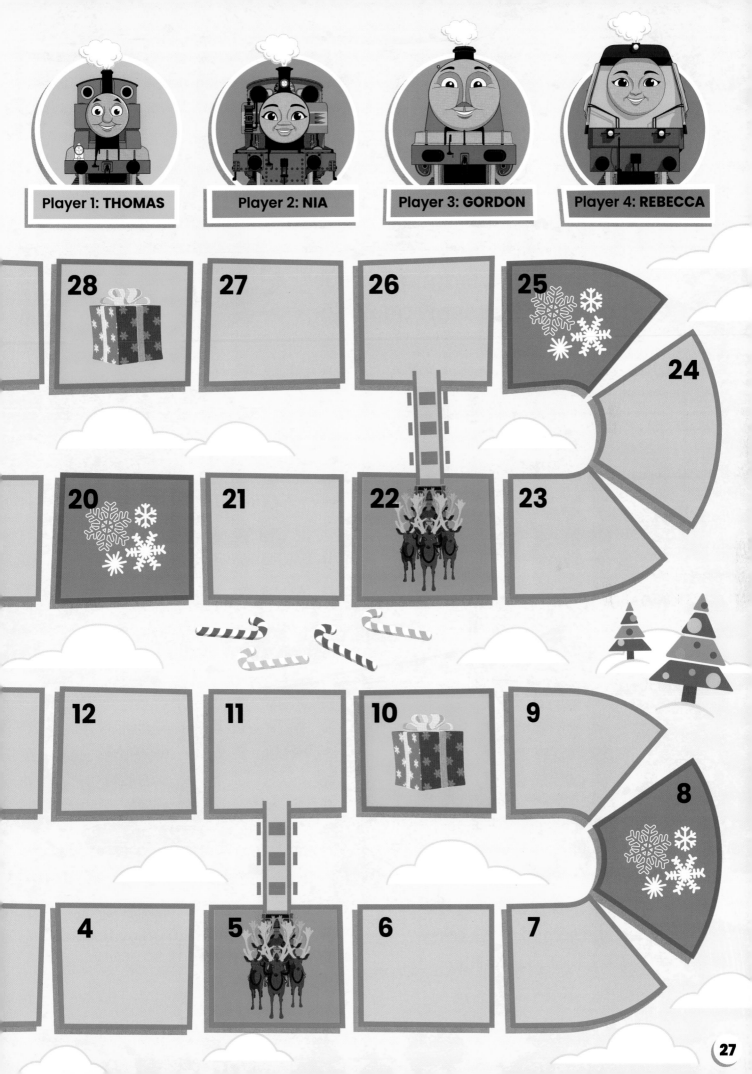

Cleo's First Snow

Read along and learn all about Cleo and her first snow on Sodor.

When Cleo woke up one morning, Sodor was covered in snow.

"What's all that fluffy stuff?" she gasped.

"That's snow," smiled Ruth. "Enjoy it while it lasts."

But Cleo wasn't so sure.

Cleo felt a bit scared of the snow.

"Don't worry, that's just a little snowman," Ruth said.

Slowly, Cleo started to enjoy the snow. Maybe it wasn't so scary after all. Whee!

But later that day, the snow started to disappear! "I'm afraid snow melts in the sun," Ruth told Cleo.

Poor Cleo didn't want the snow to melt. "I'll save you, snowman!"

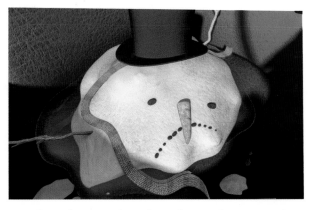

By the time Cleo had got home, the snowman had completely melted.

"Oh no!" sobbed Cleo. "I'm going to miss the snow so much."

This gave Ruth an idea ...

The next morning, Cleo woke up to another surprise.

Ruth had made a snow machine, just for Cleo.

Now Cleo could enjoy snow every day. "I love it," giggled Cleo. "Snow forever!"

Surprise Cargo

James is bringing an important delivery to a party.
Can you pile the flatbed high with party cargo?

You could draw balloons, presents, lights, cakes ... anything you like!

Count Along

Use a pencil to race through Kenya with Nia. Count the different types of animals and point to your answers in the numberline.

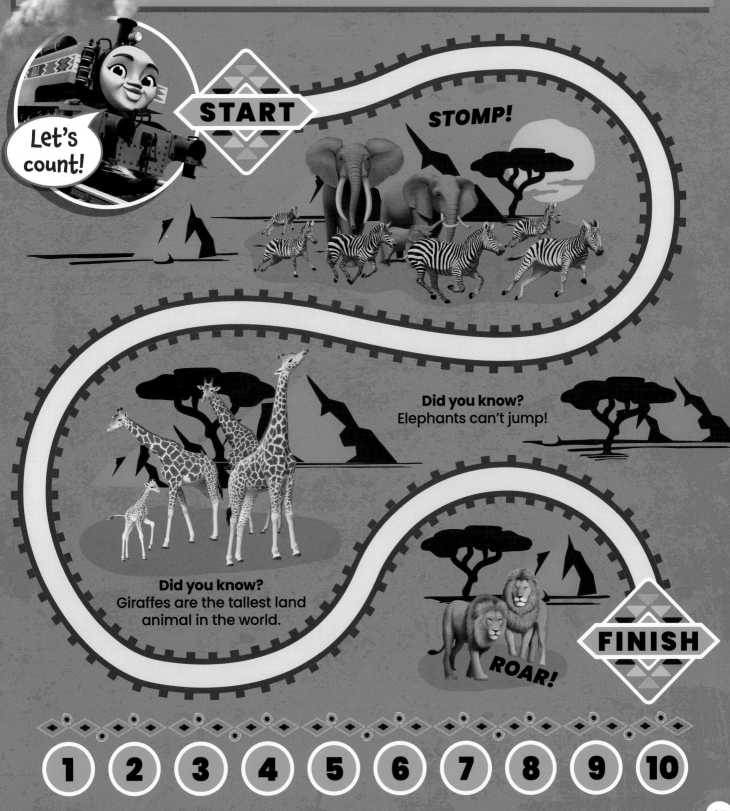

Paint Workshop

It's time for a quick stop at the workshop.
Use your crayons to give James a shiny, new paint job.
Use the coloured dots to help you.

Make me splendid!

Now trace over his number on the side.

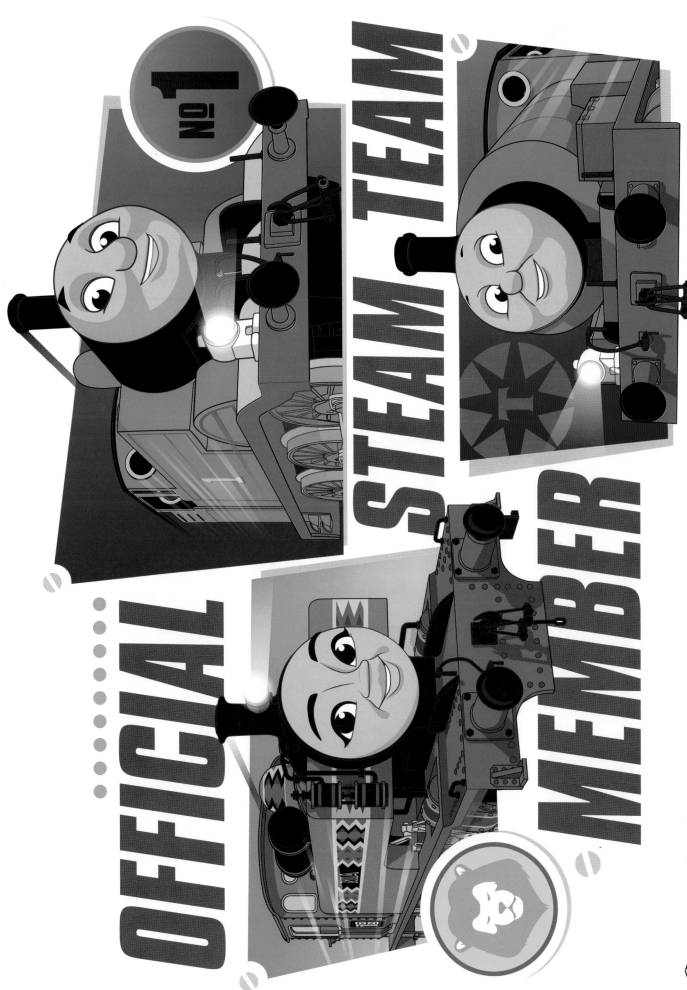

© 2022 Gullane (Thomas) Limited
© 2022 HIT Entertainment Limited.

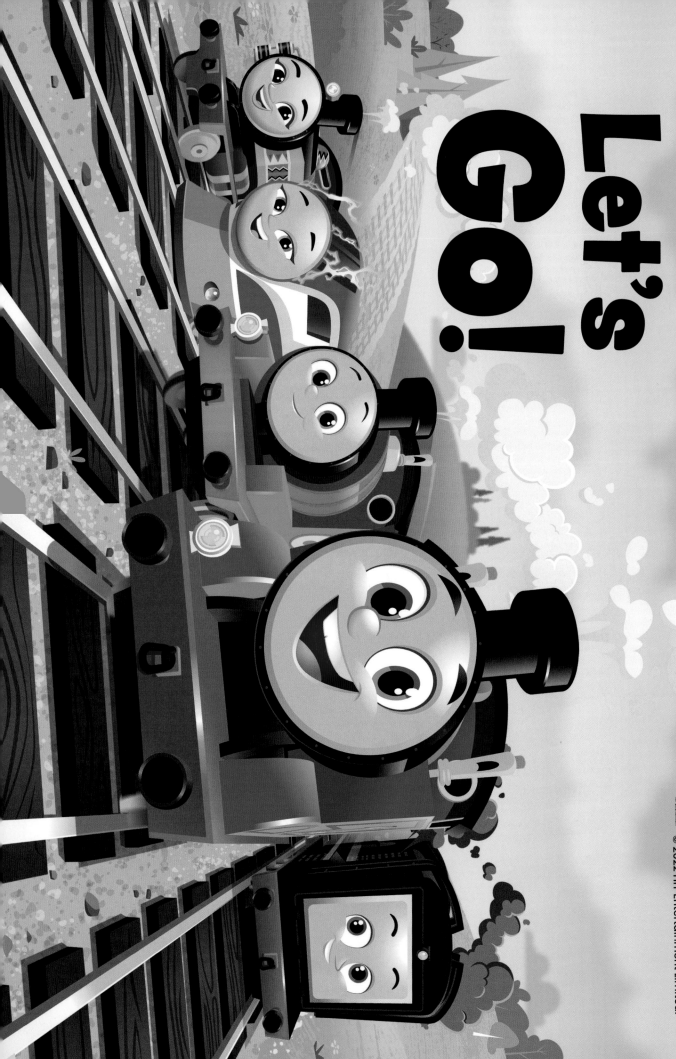

Let's Go!

 © 2022 Gullane (Thomas) Limited
© 2022 HIT Entertainment Limited.

New Adventures

Thomas and Percy are ready for some new adventures.
Colour the picture so they can get started.
Peep! Peep!

Here Come the Engines!

Read all about your favourite friends before they race off down the rails. Can you point to your favourite engine?

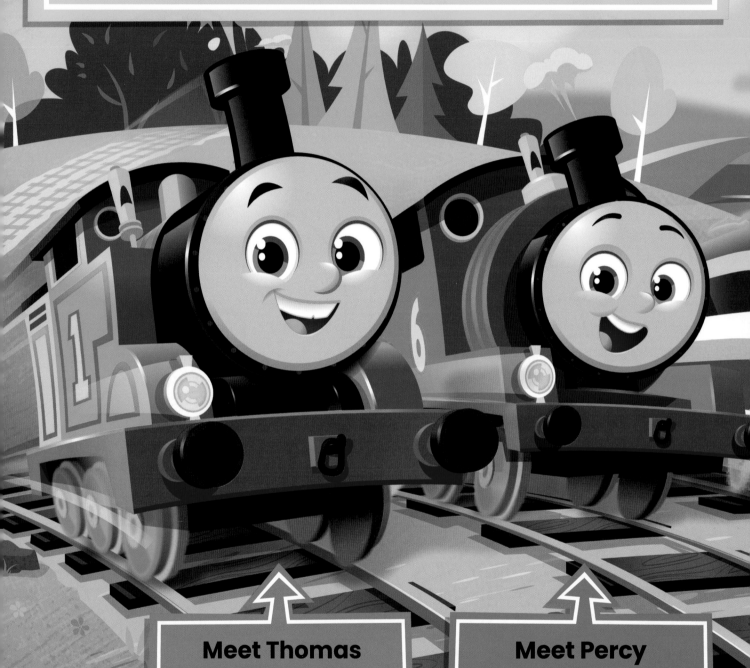

Meet Thomas

The Number 1 Engine spins, flips and jumps around Sodor with his friends. When there is adventure to be found, Thomas is there!

Meet Percy

This little green engine loves to make his friends giggle. He sometimes needs help from the bigger engines, but he tries hard at everything he does.

ALL ENGINES GO™

Meet Kana
Kana is the first electric engine to live on Sodor. She speeds from place to place in a gust of wind. Whoosh!

Meet Nia
Nia has a clever plan for every problem. When she is not helping her friends, she is bop-bop-bopping to her favourite music.

Meet Diesel
Cheeky Diesel brings fun and trouble wherever he goes. He always wants to win, even if that means making more mischief!

A Thomas Promise

One morning, Thomas was showing his friends how high he could stack some **wibbly-wobbly** tracks.

"I'll bet I can go higher," said Diesel. He tried to pull the flatbed from Thomas.

"No you can't, because I'm the Number 1 Engine!" Thomas clung onto his tracks.

Heave, pull, heave!

"Oh dear!"

CRASH! The little tracks flew all over the rails, just as Gordon whizzed into view. Poor Gordon jumped and landed with a **BUMP!**

Gordon's coupling had snapped in two.

"How am I going to take my cargo to Whiff's Recycling Plant now?" steamed Gordon.

"Well, I can take half and Diesel can take half," said Thomas. "It's a Thomas Promise!"

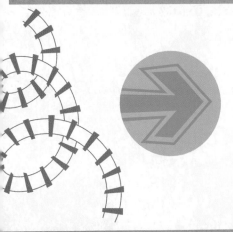

Gordon agreed, and the engines set off.

"Do you want to race?" Thomas asked Diesel. "Last one to Whiff's Recycling Plant is a rotten rail spike."

Now Thomas could show Diesel that he really was the Number 1 Engine!

Thomas's wheels turned *faster, faster, faster*. But he skidded onto the wrong side track.

"Woah!" Thomas cried. He leaped over Kana, just in time.

Bump! Bump! Gordon's cargo tumbled onto the tracks. Thomas felt silly for going so fast, but he still wanted to win the race.

When the cargo was back on board, Thomas steamed off to catch up to Diesel.

"Time for a track attack," said Thomas. But sneaky Diesel had another plan ...

He quietly flipped some of his heavy cargo into Thomas' trucks. Now Thomas' cargo was heavier than ever.

Puff, puff, puff! Poor Thomas couldn't pull his trucks for another second.

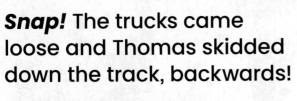

Snap! The trucks came loose and Thomas skidded down the track, backwards!

Up ahead, the tracks were all broken up. With a flip and a flop, Thomas spun in the air and landed with a ...

... **SPLAT!** Thomas was stuck in a very muddy bog.

Luckily, Sandy, Carly and Percy soon arrived to pull Thomas out.

"I guess I'm not the Number 1 Engine after all," blushed Thomas.

"You don't have to win everything to be a great engine," said Sandy.

Maybe Sandy was right. And Thomas couldn't give up on his delivery now. He still had to keep his Thomas Promise to Gordon!

Back on the rails, Diesel was causing all sorts of trouble. He was spilling Gordon's cargo everywhere.

Luckily, there was somebody on Sodor who could save the day ...

Thomas worked hard to pick up every piece of Diesel's lost cargo.

"Thomas to the rescue!"

When Thomas finally rolled into the yard, Diesel was already there.

"I won the race!" Diesel sang out. But what a shock he got when he saw that his own trucks were empty, and Thomas' were full!

"You may have arrived first, but Thomas kept his promise," said Sandy.

Thomas realised that winning wouldn't make him the Number 1 Engine, but keeping a promise definitely would!

Here Comes Thomas

Thomas is a cheeky little engine who loves big adventures. He *whizzes* and *whooshes* around Sodor finding fun and friends wherever he goes. *Peep! Peep!*

Draw puffs of steam for Thomas.

FUN FACTS

Number: 1

Colour: blue

Loves: doing jumps, flips and spins

Full steam ahead!

THOMAS

Did you know? Thomas once lost some cows on a farm delivery. **Whoops!**

Mine Maze

Thomas and Percy need to collect a lost map in the mine. But it's *spoooooooky* and dark.

START

Guide the little engines through the mine to the map. Then quickly race back out again!

FINISH

Answers on page 69.

Loop-the-Loop

Whoosh! Nia is ready for a rollercoaster ride.

Use a pencil to carefully trace her loop-the-loop track.

Let's rock and roll!

Now draw some twisty-turny tracks for Thomas.

We're on the right track!

Fast Friends

Woohoo! Kana and Diesel are having a race.
Follow the lines to find out who gets to the FINISH first,
and who gets stuck in a muddy puddle.

START

Kana

Diesel

It's taking part that counts!

Now use your best crayons to colour a trophy for each racer.
Well done, team!

FINISH

Here Comes Percy

Percy worries about lots of things, but he can also be super brave. If his friends are in trouble, he will face his fears to help them. With Thomas by his side, he can do anything!

This is going to be epic!

FUN FACTS

Number: 6

Colour: green

Best friend: Thomas

Loves: his lucky bell. Ding-a-ling!

Did you know? Percy is scared of the dark.

PERCY

Thomas helping Percy in the dark!

Party Time

Percy is getting ready for a big party on Sodor.
Can you find the close-ups in the big picture?

*Colour in Percy's party balloon
when you have found them all.*

Thomas Blasts Off

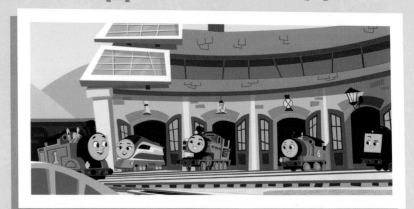

Today was the day of the big rocket launch on Sodor. All the engines were so excited to see a rocket fly.

"Prepare to blast off!" peeped Thomas.

But when the engines got to Knapford Station, the rocket was in pieces.

"The rocket fell apart!" gasped Percy.

Gordon chuckled. "No, no. It's just too big to deliver in one piece," he said. "You will all have to take it to Brendam Docks in small pieces."

"**Woohoo!**" the engines cheered. Now they were even more excited. They got to deliver a real-life rocket!

Nia took the shell of the rocket. "Toot-ally awesome!"

Kana took the booster. "That's what makes it go, go, go!"

Diesel took the wings. "Now it can fly!"

What part could Thomas deliver?

All that was left was a tiny battery.

"B-b-but I wanted to take a big part, like everyone else," said Thomas. "This is teeny-weeny."

Gordon told Thomas that the battery was very important, but Thomas felt disappointed.

Thomas looked at his little battery. He knew he should take his delivery, but he really wanted to race next to the exciting rocket parts.

"Thomas to lead our space convoy to Planet Brendam Docks!" Thomas giggled.

The battery could wait until later.

When the engines arrived at the launch site, Cranky was not happy.

"Where is the battery?" he asked.

"The battery! I'll be back in a sonic boom!" said Thomas, quickly.

Whoosh!

Thomas hadn't got far when he saw Kana with her booster. She was stuck in mud.

Thomas kindly stopped to push Kana until she was back on track.

"We have lift off!" Thomas cried out.

Thomas raced back to the docks with Kana. He wanted to tell everyone how he had helped with the big rocket booster.

Cranky was not impressed. "Erm, but I also ordered a battery, Thomas ..." he grumbled.

"Uh oh," said Thomas. "Blasting off for battery recovery mission!"

As Thomas rattled off down the rails, thunder rumbled in the distance.

"I just hope Thomas gets the battery back before it rains," Cranky said. "Or the launch will be cancelled."

Thomas was determined not to stop this time, but Gordon was in trouble.

"The wind knocked a tree onto my coupler," said Gordon. "Can you take the rocket's nose for me?"

"Abso-TOOT-ley!" Finally, Thomas got to deliver a big rocket part.

Thomas proudly rolled back into the docks. But not everybody was happy with Thomas.

"Where is your battery? The rocket can't take off without it," said Cranky. "Your battery powers everything."

Thomas blushed. He had spent so much time helping with the big deliveries, he hadn't done his own job.

Thomas whooshed off as fast as his little wheels would go. All the while, thunder rumbled in the distance.

"I've got to beat the storm!" Thomas puffed.

This time, Thomas didn't stop or get distracted. He picked up his battery and got his delivery back on track. But the storm was getting stronger.

Wind whipped down the tracks. Rocks crashed into poor Thomas.

"Woah ... c-c-can't stop!" Thomas called out. He was picking up speed.

Thomas whizzed like a rocket towards the launch site. Suddenly, the battery flew off the flatbed, spun into the air, and landed ...

... right inside the rocket!

Kana hit the launch button. *3, 2, 1 ... blast off!*

Boom!
The rocket shot up into the stormy sky.

"You did it, Thomas! You saved the launch," said Gordon. "You mean my little battery did," smiled Thomas.

From now on, Thomas promised to take every delivery he was given. No matter how big or small a job might seem, every job is important on Sodor.

Peep! Peep!

Rocket Ready

Let's get ready for blast off!
Use a pencil to trace over the dots to make
a big rocket. Now add lots of colours.

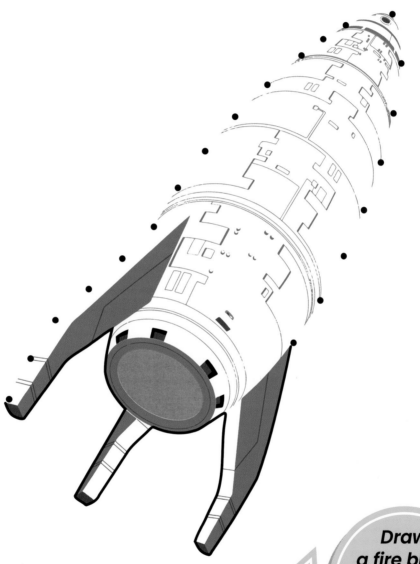

Draw a fire blast at the bottom of the rocket. Boom!

Here Comes Sandy

Sandy may be small but she is mighty. If an engine is in trouble, Sandy is ready to save the day. This little rail speeder is not afraid to get her wheels dirty!

I'll make your problems disappear!

SANDY

FUN FACTS

Super skill: she can squeeze into small, tricky places

Job: to fix broken parts

Loves: playing in sand

Did you know? Sandy likes to have mud fights

Sandy and her messy play!

What a Mess!

Splat! Sandy is spraying mud everywhere!
Draw lines to take each muddy friend through the
bubbly washdown to the matching clean friend.

1

2

3

4

5

a

b

c

d

e

Chasing Rainbows

Listen to this story all about a rainbow on Sodor.
When you see a picture, join in and say the word.

 rainbow    rain    Thomas   Kana   mountain

It was a grey day on Sodor. and were

playing in the . *Splish, splash, splosh!*

When the sun finally came out again, something amazing

appeared in the sky. "A !" said .

"Do you think there is treasure at the end of the ?"

 wasn't sure, so they set off to find out.

They chased the all over Sodor.

No matter how close they got,

the ran away!

All the engines came to help, but nobody could catch

the . Suddenly, 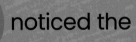 noticed the dip behind

a big, strange .

Quick as a flash, the friends whirred round and round the

 . When they reached the top, the started to

disappear. felt sad. Then he noticed an entrance to

a secret station.

"Look!" gasped . "This can be our secret club house

for our Biggest Adventure Club!"

The engines cheered. "We might not

have reached the end of the ,

but we have found some treasure,"

giggled . *Treasure for us all to share!*

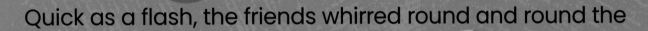

Here Comes Kana

Whoosh! Kana thinks fast, talks fast and moves fast. Her super electric speed means she travels so fast, she can sometimes cause chaos!

Let's fast track this!

KANA

FUN FACTS

Rail power: electricity

Colour: purple

Loves: going faster than everyone else

Did you know? Kana needs to keep her electric power charged up

Kana getting all charged up!

Flip, Fizz, Flash!

Kana is *fizzing* with electricity today. Use the little picture of Kana to help you colour in the big picture. Now draw flashes of electricity to make Kana *go, go go!*

Rocking Rails

Peep! Peep!
Percy and Nia are having a race around Sodor.
Can you spot five differences in picture b?

Colour in an engine each time you find a difference.

Busy-whizzy Day

Come along and join Thomas' very busy day, from morning to night. Use your finger to travel around Sodor, taking the challenges along the way.

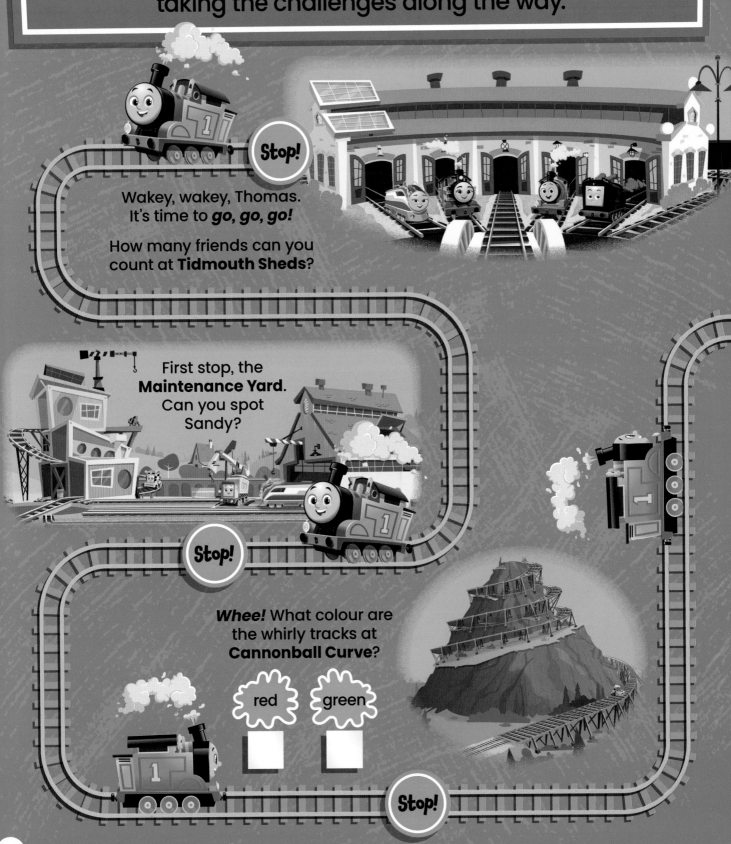

Stop!

Wakey, wakey, Thomas. It's time to *go, go, go!*

How many friends can you count at **Tidmouth Sheds**?

First stop, the **Maintenance Yard.** Can you spot Sandy?

Stop!

Whee! What colour are the whirly tracks at **Cannonball Curve**?

red   green

Stop!

McColls farm is noisy today.

Can you make the sound of a sheep?

Stop!

Let's wave to **Sir Topham Hatt.**

Stop!

What a busy day. Say 'Night, night!' to Thomas.

Stop!

Count the pretty butterflies!

Can you stop to trace over this butterfly?

Stop!

See You Soon!

Grab your best crayons and colour
this happy Sodor picture.
Bye-bye, Steam Team!

Answers

Page 8

Page 11

Page 12

1 = Rebecca, 2 = Thomas
3 = Percy, 4 = Emily

Page 20

1 = Dog, 2 = Branch
3 = Squirrel, 4 = Little boy

Page 22

Page 31

There are:
6 zebras, 3 elephants,
4 giraffes and 2 lions.

Page 45

Page 47

Kana wins the race.

Page 49

Page 59

1) c = Thomas
2) d = Percy
3) e = Sandy
4) a = Diesel
5) b = Kana

Page 64

Page 66

• There are 4 friends at
  Tidmouth Sheds.
• The tracks at Cannonball
  Curve are red.
• There are 7 pretty
  butterflies.